Little Legends
THE SPELL THIEF

TOM PERCIVAL

Little Legends

THE SPELL THIEF

sourcebooks
jabberwocky

Published by Sourcebooks Jabberwocky, an imprint of Sourcebooks, Inc.
P.O. Box 4410, Naperville, Illinois 60567-4410
(630) 961-3900
Fax: (630) 961-2168
www.sourcebooks.com

Originally published in 2016 in the United Kingdom by Macmillan Children's Books, an imprint of Pan Macmillan.

Library of Congress Cataloging-in-Publication Data

Names: Percival, Tom, 1977- author.
Title: The spell thief / Tom Percival.
Description: Naperville, Illinois : Sourcebooks Jabberwocky, [2016] | Series: Little legends ; 1 | Summary: "Jack (of the beanstalk fame) and his magical talking chicken, Betsy, have always been great at making new friends, like their BFFs Red and Rapunzel. But when Jack spots Anansi, the new kid in town, talking to a troll in the Deep Dark Woods, everything changes. Everyone knows that trolls mean trouble, and Jack will do anything to prove to the rest of his friends that Anansi is a troll spy. Even if that means using stolen magic!"-- Provided by publisher.
Identifiers: LCCN 2016004442 | (13 : alk. paper)
Subjects: | CYAC: Characters in literature--Fiction. | Friendship--Fiction. | Magic--Fiction.
Classification: LCC PZ7.P4235 Sp 2016 | DDC [Fic]--dc23 LC record available at https://lccn.loc.gov/2016004442

Source of Production: Versa Press, East Peoria, Illinois, USA
Date of Production: October 2016
Run Number: 5007560

Printed and bound in the United States of America.
VP 10 9 8 7 6 5 4 3 2 1

*This book is dedicated to Sheila Percival—
for opening my eyes to the wonder of stories.
Thanks, Mum!*

Contents

I

A Ship Comes In

*J*ack walked through the Deep Dark Woods with his pet hen Betsy tucked under one arm. He took a deep breath of the woodland air. It smelled fresh and exciting. Today was going to be a good day—he could just tell.

He walked toward a small, wooden cottage surrounded by a well-kept wooden fence. There was a fountain in the garden, also made of wood, but instead of water, it was blowing sawdust high into the air.

"**Whaaaat?**" squawked Betsy.

"Don't worry, Betsy. It's only sawdust," replied Jack. He wasn't surprised that his hen had just spoken to him. After all, Betsy was a magical hen. Sadly, "What?" was the only thing she could say, which made most of their conversations rather one-sided.

Jack wiped his feet on the wooden doormat and knocked on the door. He heard booming footsteps from inside. The door swung open with a creak and a very woody smell.

WHAAT!!

A large man stood in the doorway, covered in wood shavings and holding a lopsided wooden cup.

"Well, look who it is!" he exclaimed with a smile, "Come on through, Jack! Red and the others are all out back."

He ushered Jack inside, where every surface, and in fact every*thing*, seemed to be made from wood...including the carpet and the curtains.

"So, how have you been, Jack?" asked Red's dad.

"Good, thanks," replied Jack politely. "How about you?"

"Oh, good, Jack, very good!" exclaimed Red's dad. "In fact, I've just made a breakthrough!"

"A breakthrough?" asked Jack.

"With the wooden socks!" replied Red's dad.

"Don't you mean *woolen*?" countered Jack.

"Woolen socks?" repeated Red's father, as if it was the most ridiculous thing he'd ever heard, "I'm a woodcutter, Jack, not a *wool cutter!*"

"Er, right…" said Jack.

"Do you want to try them on?" asked Red's father, holding out two very solid, very wooden-looking socks.

"Um, not right now," replied Jack. "I'd better go and catch up with Red. But thanks for the offer."

———— ◆ ————

Jack raced through the house and into the garden. The tree house towered up in front of him. Red's dad had carved it out of one giant tree.

Jack's friends were all sitting in the main room when he climbed in.

"Morning, all!" he called out.

Red grinned, Rapunzel did her very best curtsy, and the twins waved enthusiastically.

PRIVAT!
CEEP OUT!

"Hey," started Hansel.
"Jack!" finished Gretel.
Hansel and Gretel often

finished each other's sentences. Sometimes it could be confusing.

"Hey, Jack!" called Red. "Do you
want the good news or the bad news?"

"The good news?" asked Jack hesitantly.

"The good news," said Rapunzel,
leaving a long pause, "is that there's a ship
coming into town from Far Far Away!"

"Whaaat?!?!" squawked Betsy.

Jack gasped. A boat from Far Far Away!
His dad might have sent him a letter…

"Yep!" added Red. "It should be arriv-
ing any minute! We're going to have

a race up to Lookout Point to watch it come in—last one there is a smelly troll!"

"So what's the bad news?" asked Jack.

"The bad news is that Hansel's just tied your shoelaces together!" said Rapunzel, as she and everyone else scrambled excitedly from the tree house.

2

A Mysterious Visitor

*B*y the time Jack had untied his laces, everyone else was out of sight. Still, he was a lot faster than his friends and sure he'd be able to make the time up— especially if he took some shortcuts.

It wasn't long before Jack was running across Market Square in the middle of town. Growing in the very center was the Story Tree that gave Tale Town its name.

The Story Tree was utterly unique. It literally grew stories—or rather, it recorded them. Every time a new story was told beneath its branches, it would sprout a tiny silver shoot, sometimes growing into a whole new branch if the story was big and exciting enough. If you ran your fingers along the tree it felt as though the stories were happening *inside* your head. Jack already had one story growing there—about the time he met a terrifying giant—and he hoped that one day he'd get another one up there.

Jack ran past the Story Tree and over to the far side of Market Square.

"Hi, Humpty!" called Jack as he ran past an egg-shaped figure perched on the edge of the town well.

"Who's there?" gasped Humpty, spinning around.

"It's just me," began Jack.

But Humpty's sudden movement caused him to wobble. His arms and legs flailed wildly, and then he fell down the well with a shriek, followed by a loud splash.

Jack stopped running and inched closer to the well. "Humpty? Are you OK?" he asked.

"Yes…" echoed a voice from far below.

"Do you want me to fetch the king's men?" asked Jack.

"Would you?" replied Humpty. "Thanks, Jack! Don't bother with any of the horses though. I don't know why anyone would think that a horse could help put an egg back together—they don't even have hands!"

"Er, no…" replied Jack. "Right, well, I'll go and get help then. I'll be as fast as I can."

———— ◆ ◆ ————

By the time Jack had run to the palace, found the king's men, and explained where Humpty was, he knew he'd lost the race, but he decided to run to Lookout Point anyway.

"You wait here, Betsy," said Jack, placing her by the palace gates. "I'm already late and…well, I can run faster on my own, OK?"

"Whaaat…" squawked Betsy sadly.

"Good girl!" said Jack, patting her on the head. "See you in a bit. Now don't go wandering off."

Even though Jack sprinted all the way up to Lookout Point, he still wasn't out of breath. But he *was* the last one of his friends to get there.

"What kept you, Jack?" asked Red.

"Jack's a troll! Jack's a troll!" called out Rapunzel, and everyone laughed.

Jack felt his ears turn red, and a hot anger swirled up inside him. He hated being called a troll. The trolls and the people of Tale Town were bitter enemies— although nobody could remember *exactly* why. Still, if it wasn't for the trolls, his dad wouldn't have to work in the mine where they dug out the brightly glowing Moonstone.

There was something in Moonstone that scared trolls away and weakened their magic. It was the only protection that the people of Tale Town had. The only place you could mine it was on the scattered islands of Far Far Away, more than three months away by boat, and *that* was why Jack hardly ever saw his dad.

"I'm no troll!" shouted Jack, more crossly than he meant to.

Everyone was silent for a moment, then Hansel called out, "Hey! Look—"

"—over there!" finished Gretel.

Sailing into harbor was a large ship flying the flag that linked Tale Town with Far Far Away.

As Jack looked down he noticed a sudden movement halfway up the ship's main mast. There was someone climbing up it. "Hey, look down there!" he said.

"What is it?" asked Red.

"I think—"

"—it's a—"

"—boy!" added Hansel and Gretel.

Jack squinted over. They were right: it *was* a boy! He was about their age, with dark skin and black hair. He climbed so quickly it looked unnatural. Once he'd reached the top of the mast, he flung out one arm and leaped into thin air.

Rapunzel gasped, but instead of falling, the boy appeared to swing on an invisible rope, far above the heads of the crowd on the dockside. He landed safely on the shore, then jogged along the path that ran directly below Lookout Point.

"Who is he, and why's he sneaking around like that?" said Jack.

"We need to find out—"

"—but how do we get—"

"—down there?" asked the twins, peering over the cliff's edge.

"I'm waaaay ahead of you guys," called Rapunzel. She unbraided her hair and let it tumble down the cliff. "Last one down's a smelly troll!"

Jack leaped forward and slid down Rapunzel's hair to the path below.

Rapunzel frowned for a moment, then said, "No, wait. Not last one—that would be me! *First* one down's a smelly troll!"

"That's *not* fair!" shouted Jack from the bottom of the cliff.

3
Web of Distrust

*O*nce everyone had climbed down, Rapunzel wrapped her hair around a tree trunk and swung down to the path in seconds. With a quick shake of her head, her hair released the trunk and tied itself into a neat braid behind her.

"Your hair is *amazing!*" said Red.

"I know," replied Rapunzel with a grin.

Staying out of sight, the five friends followed the mysterious boy as he darted through the woods toward Tale Town.

"He's so fast!" exclaimed Red.

"He's not *that* fast…" muttered Jack, although he was starting to feel a little tired out. Before long, everyone else had fallen behind, and it was just Jack and Red chasing the distant figure.

Suddenly, the boy shot upward into the leaves of an overhead tree.

"Hey!" said Red, skidding to a halt. "Where did he go?"

"I don't know," whispered Jack, his heart pounding in his ears.

A twig snapped, and the two friends spun around.

There was the boy they'd been chasing!

He was leaning against a tree behind them, twiddling a leaf between his fingers.

"So," said the boy, a confident smile flashing across his face, "I was just wondering, why are you following me?"

"I...well...we were...I mean..." Red looked over to Jack for help.

Jack narrowed his eyes. "Why were you sneaking off that boat?" he asked.

"Good question!" exclaimed the boy. "Maybe I'm a stowaway. Or it could be that I'm a visiting prince from a distant land, sent here to buy your town! Or perhaps I'm just staying here on vacation with my uncle. You can decide which!"

At that moment, Rapunzel, Hansel, and Gretel burst into the clearing, puffing and panting.

"What…?" exclaimed Rapunzel.

"Who…?" began Hansel.

"We don't know!" said Jack. "That's exactly the point! Who are you?"

"Oh, that's easy!" replied the boy. "I'm me, of course, which means that you must be you, and these people here"—he pointed at Red, Rapunzel, and the twins—"must be them. So, now that we're all friends, how about you show me the quickest way into town?"

Red and Rapunzel smiled, but Jack was still looking sternly at the boy.

"Come on, Jack!" said Red. "Give him a chance." She turned to face the stranger. "I'm Red, this is Rapunzel, the twins are Hansel and Gretel, and our grumpy friend here is Jack."

Jack sighed. There was something about this boy that made him feel uneasy, but he didn't want to upset Red. He looked at his feet, lifted one hand, and muttered, "All right."

"Well, seeing as we're doing things properly," said the boy, "my name is Anansi. I come from Far Far Away, and I'm staying here with my uncle for a vacation. Nice to meet you—*all* of you," he added with a grin, looking Jack straight in the eye.

"Nice to meet you too," said Red. "So, how did you manage to climb that tree so fast?"

Anansi grinned.
"With a little help from
my friends!" He raised his
arms and made a funny clicking
noise in the back of his throat. Two
large spiders dropped down from the
branches above on delicate lines of spider
silk. Anansi grabbed hold of the narrow
threads and with a flick of his wrists was
sent flying up into the treetops.

"Whoa! Now—" said Hansel.

"—that was cool," finished Gretel.

Jack nodded to himself. It *was* pretty cool. He peered up into the leaves and was surprised to see a small imp straddling a branch. Imps didn't usually venture this close to Tale Town. They lived out in the dark, gloomy forests a few miles to the west. They weren't evil, but could often be mean-spirited and untrustworthy. Jack was just about to point the imp out to the others, when he saw that Anansi was on the same branch and was saying something to it.

Jack squinted more closely. Anansi nodded his head and the imp leaped away, its tiny body scampering easily over the narrow branches.

"Did anyone else see that?" exclaimed Jack, looking around at his friends. But nobody was listening. They were all staring up as Anansi lowered himself from the branches. He was hanging upside down from one tiny, almost invisible thread.

"Is that—"

"—magic?" whispered Hansel and Gretel.

Anansi laughed his warm, friendly laugh. "I don't think so. I've always been able to do it. Spiders just seem to like me." He made the clicking noise in the back of his throat again, and the clearing filled with all sorts of spiders that scuttled toward him.

"Wow!" murmured Red.

"Wait a minute!" said Jack. "Seriously… did no one else see what just happened?"

"Yeah," said Red. "Pretty cool, eh?"

"No!" said Jack. "I'm not talking about your new best friend's spider tricks! I'm talking about him having a cozy little chat with an imp up there in the treetops."

"What?" asked Red, her eyes wide. Jack nodded.

"An imp?" asked Anansi. "Where? I've never seen one before."

"Don't play tricks with me!" said Jack. "I saw you up there."

"All the way up there?" asked Anansi.

"Through all those branches and all those leaves? You've got good eyesight, Jack!"

"I know what I saw!" replied Jack.

"I'm sure you *think* you do," said Anansi. "But we all make mistakes. Let me introduce you to your imp." He made a soft clicking noise, and a large, friendly looking spider crept down the branch of a tree. It was the same blue-gray color as an imp and almost exactly the same size.

"I did *not* see that spider up there!" insisted Jack. "It *was* an imp!"

"Oh come on, Jack!" said Rapunzel firmly. "What would an imp be doing here anyway? Unless it could smell your socks, which I know I can!"

Everyone laughed—apart from Jack.

"So, do you want us to show you around?" asked Rapunzel brightly. "My dad's kind of like the king here, so—"

"One hour—"

"—three minutes—"

"—and twenty-seven seconds!" interrupted Hansel and Gretel, both grinning.

"What are you talking about?" asked Red.

"That's how long it was since—"

"—Rapunzel last mentioned that her dad—"

"—is the king," explained the twins.

Rapunzel shot the two of them a very fierce look. "I only mentioned it so Anansi knows that nothing's off-limits!" she protested.

"Of course you did, Rapunzel," said Red. "Now, remind me...which prince was staying at your house last week? And how many horses did he give you?"

"Oh, get lost!" exploded Rapunzel as Red, Hansel, and Gretel burst out laughing.

"Well, I don't have any horses..." interrupted Anansi. "And my dad's not a king—he's a miner—but I would still like a tour of your town after I've met up with my uncle."

"Hey, Jack," said Red. "Your dad's a miner too, isn't he?"

"Yeah…" muttered Jack. "But I wish he wasn't."

Red turned back to Anansi. "We'll be in Market Square. Meet you there later?"

"OK," said Anansi. "Although I've got no idea where Market Square is!"

Red laughed. "Come on, I'll point it out on the way."

———◆◆———

There was lots of excited chatter as everyone headed off toward town—everyone except for Jack.

"Aren't you coming too, Jack?" asked Red.

"No, I'd better find Betsy," said Jack. "I promised her I wouldn't be long."

"OK, see you later then," said Red.

Jack watched as his friends walked off into the distance.

"I don't trust that boy…" he muttered quietly. He *knew* that he was right, but Red and the others hadn't seen the imp. How were they to know that Anansi was lying? And how could he make them see the truth?

4

A Secret Meeting

*B*y the time Jack got back to the palace, Betsy was nowhere to be seen. In the end, he found her by a farmer's cottage on the edge of town, her head deep in a huge bucket of grain.

The farmer was quite nice, really, but his wife was another matter. She always carried a huge old carving knife that she waved around when she got angry—and she got angry *a lot*. Nearly every mouse (blind or otherwise) within five hundred feet of their cottage was missing a tail, an ear, or in some cases, a leg. A few ex-mice were even missing heads! She had made it very clear to Jack that if she ever caught Betsy eating their corn again, the farmer would be having hen burgers for dinner.

Jack tiptoed into the garden, grabbed Betsy, and slipped quietly away.

As they walked back into town, Jack told Betsy about what had happened in the woods.

"Honestly, Betsy," he said, "I swear I saw Anansi talking to an imp in that tree!"

"Whaaat!"

"Exactly! That's just what I said."

"Whaaaat?"

"Nope. None of them believed me—not even Red. She thinks I'm just being mean."

"Whaaat!"

"Well, yes! Of course I need proof that he's up to something! But how?"

"WhaAaa—"

Jack's hand suddenly clamped Betsy's beak shut. Her beady eyes glared up at him angrily.

"*Sorry, Betsy!*" whispered Jack. "*I can see Anansi just ahead!*"

"**Whaaaat?**" said Betsy very quietly.

"Yes…" muttered Jack. "He *is* on his own."

Jack hid behind a large barrel and peered around it, trying to see what Anansi was up to.

The boy was sitting on a bench by the woods to the west of Tale Town, leaning back as though he was trying to look relaxed. Jack watched and waited. He didn't know what he was waiting for. It was just that something didn't feel right.

Nothing happened.

Jack's legs were getting pins and needles, but still he waited. He waited for so long that he started to wonder if he might have been wrong. He was just trying to figure out how to walk away without it looking like he'd been spying, when something finally happened.

A spider was struggling across the ground with a rolled-up piece of paper tied to its hairy back. Anansi swiftly reached down and untied the paper. He inspected it for a second, then patted the spider gently on the head, looked carefully around, then stood up and walked away.

"What's he up to now?" Jack whispered to Betsy. He waited until Anansi was almost out of sight, and then sneaked after him.

◆—◆—◆

Half an hour later, they were deep in the forest outside Tale Town. Anansi jogged quickly along the narrow paths while Jack stumbled and tripped behind him, trying to stay out of sight. Betsy was cradled under his arm, on strict instruction to stay completely silent, not to move…and basically to act like she wasn't even there.

The air in the dark woods was thick and damp. Twisted trees rose up overhead, covered in so much moss that it was hard to tell where the ground stopped and the trees began.

Anansi stopped in front of a fallen tree. The roots rose above him like huge dead claws.

Jack scrambled into a ditch to hide. He placed Betsy on the ground beside him and peered out. It wasn't long before he saw a small blue-gray shape with pointed ears scamper along the fallen tree trunk and land at Anansi's feet. Jack's eyes narrowed. It was the same imp he'd seen in the tree!

Anansi looked serious. There was no trace of the easy smile he had worn earlier. He spoke sharply to the imp in a language that Jack couldn't understand. The imp nodded, then ran out of the clearing, returning moments later with… No! It couldn't be! Jack's mouth hung open in shock.

Walking into the clearing was a troll. A huge, great, hulking beast of a thing. Just one of its hands could completely surround Jack's head, and its thick arms looked frighteningly, crushingly strong. The creature's eyes burned with darkness. Its pockmarked skin was scaly and glistened in the dim light.

Jack looked on in horror as Anansi smiled and ran forward.

"Anansi!" exclaimed the troll, in a voice like boulders being crushed together. "It's good to see a friendly face!"

"Rufaro!" said Anansi, reaching up to embrace the troll, before stepping back to regard it properly. "How have you been? You're looking good!"

For a moment the troll stared blankly

at Anansi. Then Anansi grinned and the troll's huge mouth split into a broad smile.

"Still like a joke I see?" the troll bellowed, slapping Anansi on the back so hard that the boy was jolted forward a few paces. "So, your little friend got my note to you?"

"Yes," replied Anansi. "You could have found a larger spider though—or used a smaller piece of paper. The poor thing looked exhausted!"

The troll smiled. "Now, tell me, do you have the potion? Is it safe?"

Anansi nodded and pulled out a small bottle full of a glowing silver liquid.

The troll looked pleased. "Well done, Anansi! I knew that you could do it! So,

tell me, are you alone? Did anyone see you come here?"

"No," replied Anansi with a hint of pride. "No one would have been able to keep up."

"Good lad," replied the troll with a grin. "We have a lot to discuss. To be on the safe side, I'll get the imp to cast a hiding spell."

The troll spoke a few words in the imp's language. The imp nodded and traced a shape in the air with its fingers.

Anansi and the troll continued their conversation, but with each word it was getting quieter and quieter. Jack could hardly hear anything they were saying now. The whole clearing suddenly flickered before his eyes and then vanished.

taking Anansi, the troll, and the imp
with it. It was as if the rest of the forest
had rushed in to fill the gap where the
clearing had been.

Jack stayed crouched in the ditch for a
long time, trying to make sense of what
he'd just seen.

Anansi was friends with the trolls! Or perhaps he was even a troll himself, disguised to look like a human boy? But why? Were the trolls planning *another* attempt to take over Tale Town?

Jack picked Betsy up and crept silently out of the ditch, making his way back toward town. He had to warn Red and the others that Anansi was working with the trolls—the future of Tale Town could be at stake.

Before he could do any of that though, he needed some answers, and he knew *just* the place to go to get them.

5

How to Trick a Troll

*T*he Tale Town library was silent and smelled of old books. Jack wandered along the maze of corridors, gazing at the leather-bound volumes that filled every inch of the shelves.

Magical Apples…Magical Arrows…Magical Axes—he couldn't be far from the section on *Magical Beasts*.

Jack felt Betsy wriggling around underneath his sweater. He had never read the

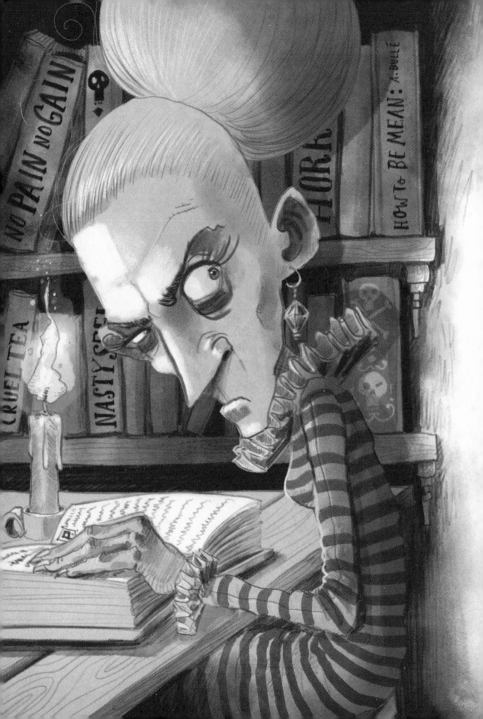

library rule book, but he was pretty sure that hens weren't welcome.

"Keep still," he muttered, earning himself a fierce look from one of the wicked stepmothers hunched over a book nearby. He wasn't sure whose wicked stepmother it was. They all looked the same: painfully thin with pointy elbows, long teeth, and mean faces.

"Be quiet, you filthy little brute!" she snapped, far louder than he had spoken to Betsy.

"I'm sorry!" replied Jack quietly.

"There you go again!" she exclaimed in horror. "Chattering away like the thoughtless creature that you are!"

Jack thought it best to say nothing and just shrugged an apology as he walked past.

"You insolent wretch!"
screeched the stepmother.
"How dare you ignore me! Why, if
you were my child I would lock you in
a cellar with no food. *That* might teach
you some manners!"

Jack rolled his eyes as he walked away.
Everyone in Tale Town knew that all
stepparents were universally awful—it
was one of the more unusual laws of the
Fairy Tale Kingdom.

Jack could still hear the wicked
stepmother ranting away when he got
to the section on *Magical Beasts*. He
pulled out a heavy book that contained

everything you could ever want to know about trolls, and a lot that you wouldn't want to—like the page that had been scented to smell exactly like a troll's breath.

Jack covered his nose and kept reading.

Troll Magick

Troll magick is much like a troll itself—crude, strong, and not very clever. However, though it be simple, their magick is VERY powerful and often goes unseen.

Jack thought about this. If Anansi *was* a troll disguised as a boy, then there was a good chance that Jack was the only one who had noticed.

There are two simple ways to break a troll spell. Firstly, make the troll angry. A troll is indeed simpleminded, and once it's angry, it's likely to forget about its spell altogether, removing whatever dark magick had been cast.

Jack nodded thoughtfully. All he had to do was make Anansi mad. Shouldn't be too difficult…

If your troll is slow to become angry, the one thing that will always break its magick is water mixed with powdered Moonstone. The soaking of a troll with this liquid will soon end its trickery.

Jack slammed the book shut. That was it! He had two foolproof methods to reveal that Anansi was a troll spy. What could possibly go wrong?

———◆◆◆———

Red, Rapunzel, and the twins were showing Anansi around Tale Town. They'd already visited Rapunzel's castle, the Singing Stream, and the Story Tree. Anansi had been telling them all about his home in Far Far Away. He was halfway through a story when Jack caught up with them.

"Hey, Jack, you have got to hear this!" exclaimed Red. "Anansi was just telling us how…"

"How he's really a troll spy?" finished Jack triumphantly.

"Umm, no…" replied Red. "How tigers have striped skin, not just striped fur."

"**Whaaat?!?!**" squawked Betsy.

"I'm not interested in any of that…" blustered Jack. "Wait a minute! Striped skin as well as fur?"

"Yeah!" replied Red.

"No way!" exclaimed Jack. "Imagine that…" Then he shook his head. "Wait, I had something important to say. Anansi *is* a troll spy, and I can prove it!"

"You can—"

"—prove it?" said Hansel and Gretel.

"I can," said Jack.

Anansi frowned.

"How?" asked Rapunzel.

"You'll see!" muttered Jack, before

spinning around to face Anansi. "So, troll boy, did you practice to get that ugly or does it just come naturally?"

"Jack!" exclaimed Red.

But Jack carried on.

"I bet your parents wanted to chop down the family tree after you were born."

"What?" asked Anansi, looking confused.

"You heard me!" repeated Jack. "Or are you dumb as well as smelly?"

"Jack!" hissed Red. "Why are you being so nasty?"

"It's OK," whispered Jack. "Trolls have

a really short temper. If I get him mad enough, he'll forget all about his spell and turn back into a troll."

Jack turned back to Anansi. "Eaten any goats recently?"

"That's enough, Jack!" shouted Rapunzel.

Red put her arm around Anansi's shoulders. "Come on," she said. "Let's

get out of here!" She glared at Jack as they walked past.

Jack frowned as everyone left. He'd explained to Red what he was trying to do. Why didn't she believe him?

"Looks like I need another plan," he muttered quietly.

"Whaaat?!?!" shrieked Betsy.

"You'll see," replied Jack, stroking the hen's head. "You'll see…"

It was early afternoon, and the sun spread a warm light all over Tale Town. Jack and Betsy were perched on a narrow roof watching the crowds pass by beneath them. Jack was balancing a small barrel of lightly glowing water between his legs.

He'd borrowed the Moonstone that his mom hung over their front door to ward off trolls and was worried that she'd find out and be angry—especially since he'd crushed it into powder and poured it into the barrel he was holding.

The more he thought about it, the more he realized it would be hard to put the Moonstone back, and therefore he hadn't really *borrowed* it at all. So he did the only thing he could and stopped thinking about it.

The plan was to wait until he saw Anansi approaching and then tip the

Moonstone water all over him, breaking the spell. Of course, the others might get a little wet too, but as soon as they saw that Anansi really was a troll, they'd forget all about it.

So Jack sat back, made himself comfortable, and waited for Rapunzel, Red, Anansi, and the twins to walk by.

———— ◆ ————

After nearly two hours, Betsy had fallen asleep, and Jack was starting to feel a lot less comfortable. It was very hot, and although he had lots of water to drink, the Moonstone made it taste really chalky. Worse than that, he needed to go to the bathroom really badly.

It was a huge relief when he finally saw

Anansi and the others walking down the alley. Jack sprang into action...or at least he tried to. He'd been sitting on the roof for so long that his legs did nothing but prickle with pins and needles. He lunged forward to try to tip the water out of the barrel, but he accidentally let go of it altogether! A sick feeling rose in his stomach as the barrel rolled down the roof and disappeared from view.

There was a scream, a shout, a splintering of wood, and a huge splash. Jack scrambled over the rooftops on clumsy legs and peered down.

There, in the middle of the alley was Anansi, stepping quickly away from the ruined remains of the barrel and the water that was already soaking into the ground.

"Did you see that?" exclaimed Rapunzel, turning with bright eyes to look at Red. "If Anansi hadn't moved so quickly, that barrel would have fallen right on top of you both!"

"I know!" gasped Red. "Thanks, Anansi!"

"I'm just glad I was able to help," said Anansi. "Now, weren't you going to show me a stall that sells singing harps?"

"Of course—"

"—come on!" replied the twins, and off they all went.

———◆———

Jack let out a huge sigh of relief. It had nearly all gone horribly wrong! But as the group walked away, Anansi spun around and glared directly at Jack. Jack ducked immediately, but he *knew* that Anansi had seen him.

Jack gently nudged Betsy, who woke and murmured, "Whaaaat?"

"No, it didn't work," replied Jack. "But we'll get him, Betsy, don't you worry about that!"

6

Cave of the Sea Witch

$\mathcal{J}$ack walked along the coastal path with Betsy under one arm. Tiny droplets of sea spray speckled his face. Even though the sun was shining, he still felt irritated. Nothing was going right.

With a yell, he grabbed a stone and flung it out to sea as far as he could. Ripples radiated from where the stone had splashed, but instead of dying away, they grew larger and larger, forming tall waves that rushed outward in a huge circle.

One moment, Jack was staring out at a calm and peaceful sea. The next, it had transformed into an angry mass of water, swirling furiously closer and closer to the shore.

Jack stepped backward as a wall of water suddenly towered above him. He turned to run, but it was too late. The next thing he knew, waves were crashing down all around him, and he was tumbling through the churning water. Jack's ears popped as he was dragged far beneath the surface. He fought to hold his breath, but he couldn't go on much longer…

"Erm, what are you doing?" asked a voice. The water had stopped swirling, but Jack still felt its cool pressure all around him.

Jack pried one eye open and saw that he was in an underwater cavern. The walls were lined with shelves holding all sorts of bottles and jars. Floating in front of him was a girl with an elegant, curling fish tail instead of legs.

"Helloooo," the girl continued, waving to get his attention. "Can you hear me?

I just wondered what you were doing with the whole scrunched-up-face thing?" She pretended that her eyes were bulging and puffed her cheeks out.

Stars pricked behind Jack's eyes. He tried to mime the need to swim to the surface and take a breath, but the girl just stared at him.

"I've never met a human before!" she continued excitedly. "Is this how you communicate? How interesting! Let me try to guess what you mean." She stared at Jack as he desperately pointed upward and then to his mouth and lungs.

"Let me see... You left your teeth above the water, and it makes your chest hurt?"

Jack shook his head furiously.

"OK, OK!" muttered the girl. "No need to get angry!"

Just as he thought he was going to pass out, Jack opened his mouth and yelled, "I'm drowning!" His voice sounded unnatural through the water, all bubbly and muted.

"You *can* speak!" exclaimed the girl brightly. "What's 'drowning'?"

Jack rolled his eyes. Just his luck—he'd been rescued by a mermaid who didn't even know what drowning was. Then he realized that there had been no rush of water into his lungs. In fact, he felt... nothing at all! He realized the awful truth. "I'm dead," he said softly.

"Whaʌaat?!" squawked Betsy's voice from behind him.

"Dead?" The girl laughed. "No, you're definitely not dead, and neither is your weird pet thing." She pointed at Betsy, who was busily pecking at some sea snails.

Jack frowned. "So…how come I can breathe down here?"

"That's easy! Magic!"

"Well, how did I get down here in the first place?"

"Magic!"

"And how can I talk when there's no air?"

"I'll give you one guess," said the mermaid.

"OK, but—"

"Look," replied the girl. "I'm a sea witch, OK?" She curled a strand of hair around one finger, then added, "Well, I work *for* a sea witch, and she's sort of training me, but I can do *some* magic of my own." With a flick of her tail, she shot through the water, coming to a stop inches away from Jack. "My name's Lily…or Lil, whichever you like. What's yours?"

"I'm Jack," he replied. "And this is my hen, Betsy."

"How *wonderful* it is to meet you both! So, what can I do for you today?"

"Sorry?"

"Well, you threw a magic stone into the sea, summoning a sea witch, so it's kind of traditional that we do a deal now. You get a spell that you think will give you everything you want…but it's basically just a mean trick that always backfires."

"Oh, right," said Jack. "That doesn't sound too great."

Lily looked worried. "My boss would be furious if she knew I'd told you that. It's a good job she's away harvesting ingredients this week."

"Ingredients?"

"Yeah, you know, tears, sorrow, first-born children—that sort of thing."

"Okaaaaay," replied Jack. "So, this is a magic shop? You sell spells?"

"Yes!" said Lily proudly. "But like I said, all sea witches' spells are kind of mean, and you and your hen thing seem so nice…"

"What are the safest, least-nasty spells you have?" Jack asked thoughtfully.

Lily's face brightened. "The nice ones are usually pretty safe. You know, spells to make you brave, kind, truthful—that sort of thing."

"You have a spell that can make you tell the truth?" asked Jack.

"Yep!" replied Lily with a smile. "Do you want to buy it?"

"Ah," said Jack, "well, I would, but I don't actually have any money."

"What's money?" asked Lily.

"This is a shop!" exclaimed Jack. "How do you sell things if you don't use money?"

Lily's eyes twinkled. "We

do things like take your soul, shorten your life by ten years, swap a spell for your laugh. You know, the usual."

"Riiight…" replied Jack. "Maybe I'll leave it for today."

"It's *such* a lovely spell!"

"I'm sure it is, but I like my laugh."

"What about your hen thing? Would you trade that?"

"WHAAAAAT!?!" squawked Betsy.

"No way!" cried Jack.

"A leg?" Lily went on.

"I don't think so."

"Arm?"

"Nope."

"Finger?"

Jack looked thoughtfully at his hands and then slowly shook his head.

"A happy memory?"

"No. Wait, what do you mean?"

"Oh, it's easy. You think of something happy, and I pluck it out of your head and bottle it. Simple as that," said Lily.

"Does it hurt?"

"You won't even know it's gone."

Jack thought about it for less than a second. "OK, I'll do it."

Lily quicky swam around the cavern three times in a row. "Oh, Jack! You've made me *so* happy! My first day alone in the shop, and I've already sold a spell! I knew I'd make a good sea witch! OK then, ready?"

It was his birthday, and he was wobbling along the lane outside his house on a wooden bike. His dad's hand was warm on his back.

"You're still holding me, aren't you?" asked Jack nervously.

"Of course!" replied his father.

Jack picked up speed.

"Still holding me?" Jack asked.

"Yes!" came his father's voice as they sped down the path and around the bend into the woods.

"Still got me?" asked Jack.

Jack's father laughed as he ran alongside his son, eyes shining in the afternoon sunlight. "I let go as soon as you started pedaling! You did that all on your own, Jack!"

"How does this work, then?" Jack asked.

"It's already done," said Lily with a sad look in her eyes. "I wish you hadn't chosen that one though. It was lovely."

"What was?" asked Jack.

"Never mind," replied Lily. "I suppose I should give you your spell now." She shot around the room, rummaging through the hundreds of bottles. "Aha!" she cried eventually, whirling around with a small, turquoise bottle.

"Now, this spell is simple. All you have to do is drink it and then everything you say for fifteen minutes can only be the truth. Pretty clever, eh?"

"Er…yeah," replied Jack, thinking he probably shouldn't say what he was really planning to use the spell for.

"So, I guess this is where we say good-bye?" said Lily.

"But we've only just met!"

"You've got about fifteen seconds before you start doing that 'drowning' thing again," explained Lily. "My magic isn't as strong as a real sea witch."

"Will I be able to come back?" asked Jack as the water began to swirl around him once more.

"Find a stone shaped like a swan," shouted Lily over the roaring water.

Betsy paddled frantically over to Jack, who pulled her tight.

"Then what?" shouted Jack.

"Same as before. Throw it into the sea," called Lily. Then she disappeared in a storm of bubbles.

7
Too Much Truth

Red, Rapunzel, Anansi, and the twins were walking through the sunshine toward Greentop's Café. Albertus Greentop made the best milk shakes in the kingdom—you could try anything from a Moonlit Rainbow to a Hint of Morning Frost, and they actually *tasted* like those things.

It wasn't just the drinks that were unusual. The café was built in the woods on platforms around a number of huge old oak trees. Steps had been carved into the trunks, and a series of bridges connected everything together. Strangest of all, its owner—Albertus Greentop—was himself a tree.

"Hey, Albie!" called out Red as they sat down at a table. "How's things?"

"Well, hello there, Miss Red!" boomed Albertus, his deep voice echoing through the clearing. "And what precisely can I effectuate for my favorite scarlet-robed heart-stealer today?"

"Pardon?" said Red.

Albertus sighed a deep, woody sigh. "What can I do for you today?"

"Ah," replied Red. "We'd like some milk shakes, please."

"Well, you've come to the right place!" exclaimed Albertus, laughing so heartily that you'd never guess he made the same joke *every* single time they visited. "What's it to be then?"

There was a rustling in the canopy

above them, and a branch bent down holding four drinks menus.

"We don't need a menu, thanks! We'll have—"

"—a G sharp and an E minor, please," said Hansel and Gretel. The twins always chose musical milk shakes. You could have an individual note, a chord, or even a full musical scale. Sometimes everyone had differ-ent musical drinks and they tried to make up a song.

"Coming right up!" Albertus

boomed once everyone else had chosen their milk shakes.

"Helloooo!" shouted an excitable voice. They all turned to see who it was.

Walking along the path toward them was a very wet-looking Jack.

"Oh, hey, Jack!" called Rapunzel. "What happened to you?"

"Hey, everyone!" Jack beamed. A crab clambered out of his pocket and hopped down to the path before scuttling back toward the sea. "I just had a quick swim. Very refreshing!"

"In your clothes?" asked Red.

"It was such a lovely day. I just couldn't wait to get in there."

"Whaʌaat?!" squawked an equally wet Betsy.

"With your hen?" asked Anansi.

"Yes! She loves swimming. Don't you, Betsy?"

Betsy didn't say anything, but her expression was not one of a hen who particularly enjoyed swimming.

"Anyway!" Jack exclaimed, putting Betsy down and clapping his hands wetly together. "How's everyone doing?"

"Good, thanks," replied Red. "You seem in a much better mood now, Jack."

"Yes, it was the swim!" said Jack, his eyes gleaming wildly. "Nothing like a bracing dip!"

"That's exactly the sort of thing my dad would say," said Rapunzel. "We've just ordered our drinks. Why don't you go and grab Albertus?"

"Terrific!" Jack grinned as he squelched off to order.

Jack was lost in a world of his own. He couldn't wait for Albertus to serve up the drinks so he could put his plan into action.

"How about you, Jack?" asked Red, looking over toward him.

"Er...yes?" said Jack, who hadn't been paying attention.

"Yes?" echoed Red, looking confused. "Rapunzel just asked what the naughtiest thing we'd ever done was?"

"Oh, right. Sorry!" replied Jack. "I never really do *anything* naughty."

"What about the time you came back down the beanstalk with *all* that giant's gold?" asked Rapunzel.

"*That* was an accident…"

"And you stole a goose—"

"—from him too!" added the twins. "You know, the one that—"

"—laid all those golden eggs."

"Well, yes, but…it just followed me home," replied Jack, feeling flustered.

Albertus called over, "Younglings, please! If you could stop your bickering for one moment, I believe your refreshments are prepared." Spindly branches parted the leaves around their table to serve up the drinks.

"Thanks, Albertus!" yelled Jack, almost jumping out of his seat in excitement. "These look delicious!"

Once everyone had their drinks in front of them, Jack waited as long as he could bear it (nearly three seconds) before he yelled, "What in the Fairy Tale Kingdom is *that*?" and pointed up into the sky.

Everyone turned to look, but there was nothing there.

By the time they had turned back, Jack had done what he needed to do and had slipped the small, turquoise bottle back into his pocket.

"What was *what*?" asked Anansi.

"Oh, nothing," replied Jack breezily. "I thought it was a dragon, but it wasn't."

"Sometimes you are just *unbelievably* odd," said Rapunzel.

"Right. Sorry!" Jack said, trying not to laugh. "I just need to… *hee hee hee!…*

ahem, use the bathroom." He raced off, letting out a loud snort of laughter as he sped away.

"I'm sorry, my charming young friends," Albertus rumbled, just after Jack had left the table. "I appear to have made a mistake with your order." Branches darted down, swapping Anansi's milk shake for Jack's. "Please accept my apologies, along with a complimentary moon muffin!"

A short while later, Jack returned looking much calmer. He sat down and took a huge gulp of his drink.

"Hmm, lovely!" he exclaimed. "How's yours, Anansi?"

"Nice, thanks," said Anansi, looking curiously at Jack.

"Excellent!" Jack clapped his hands together happily. "Now, Anansi, just remind me again, what *exactly* was it that brought you to Tale Town?"

"OK," said Anansi, frowning. "Just like I told you earlier… I'm staying here with my uncle for vacation."

Jack's eyes bulged in surprise. "That's not right! You're supposed to be telling the truth!"

"I am," replied Anansi.

"Look, why don't you join in our game?" said Red, changing the subject. "It was my turn to ask a question while you were in the bathroom, so I asked everyone about the most embarrassing thing they'd ever done. What's yours?"

Jack shrugged. He still had fifteen minutes to get the truth out of Anansi. Perhaps the spell took a little while to work?

"Last term, I called our teacher 'Mom,'" said Jack without meaning to.

His hands flew up to his mouth, but it was too late.

"Whaaat?!?!" squawked Betsy, and everybody else burst out laughing.

"That's the best yet!" laughed Rapunzel. "Anything to add to that, Jack?"

"Yes," replied Jack, although he desperately wanted to stop talking. "You know when the school toilets were clogged?"

Everyone nodded.

"It was me," wailed Jack. "I tried to flush my sandwiches away because I didn't like them, and they blocked the drain."

The roars of laughter got louder, but Jack kept on talking. He couldn't help himself.

"I once slipped over in a pile of donkey poop. I still take my teddy bear to bed with me. I'm really scared of moths, and just last week I cried when mom wouldn't let me have any pudding."

The laughter got louder and louder.

"Now *that's* embarrassing!" said Anansi. "Why are you telling us all this, Jack?"

Jack tried desperately to clamp his mouth shut. "Because I bought a truth spell from a sea witch"—he continued talking through gritted teeth—"and I put it in your drink."

The laughter stopped. Red gasped.

"Something must have gone wrong," Jack said as he stood up from the table, "and now I've drunk it instead."

"Jack!" exclaimed Rapunzel. "That must be the *meanest* thing you've ever done!"

"Maybe! But it was also me that tied your hair to a horse when we were little," blurted out Jack as he grabbed Betsy and sprinted out of Greentop's Café.

———◆———

Fifteen minutes later, Jack was back at the beach. Angry tears stung his eyes as he searched through the sand on hands and knees, desperately looking for a stone shaped like a swan.

8
Spelling Trouble

Over the next few days, Jack returned to see Lily many times. In fact, he was seeing more of her than anyone else. Every time Jack visited her, Lily traded a spell for one of his memories—but every time, *something* went wrong.

After the truth spell, Jack had tried a mind-reading spell. He'd been convinced that if he could see what Anansi was thinking, he'd be able to catch him lying.

But as it happened, he hadn't even got close to Anansi.

Lily hadn't explained that Jack would be able to read the minds of *every* single living thing.

It was just too much—hundreds of different people, all at the same time, thinking things like, "I'm hungry," or, "I feel a little tired," but usually, "Mmmm, how about a nice cup of tea?"

As if that wasn't bad enough, he could hear all the animals' thoughts too! They tended to run along the lines of, "That's a tasty-looking worm," and, "I wonder why that bird is looking at me like that," usually followed by, "Arggghhh, I'm being eaten by a bird!"

Jack had made it as far as the edge of town before he had given up and run off somewhere to be completely alone. Even then, he could hear a depressed earwig wishing that it had been born as a tiger instead.

The next spell gave Jack hypnotic powers. Lily told him that all he had to do was look into someone's eyes and they would be completely hypnotized for eight hours. Jack had gulped the potion in one foul-tasting gulp. But there was no tingling feeling, no flash of lightning or puff of smoke. As soon as his mom had left for work, he took the quickest possible peek in a mirror—just to see if he could tell if it was actually working.

Jack stared and stared at his reflection

until he didn't even feel like he was standing in front of a mirror anymore. Instead he was diving down through shining pools of light and drifting along in a warm, relaxing world with no sense of time or space.

The next thing he knew, his mom was opening the door as she came home at the end of the day. He felt incredibly hungry and had been drooling down the front of his sweater.

"Hello, Jack!" his mom called out with a smile. "You look like you've stood there all day! Make me a cup of tea, would you, love? I'm parched!"

Nearly a week had passed since Anansi first arrived in Tale Town, and Jack and Betsy had come back to see Lily *again*. He floated sadly in the underwater cave.

"I just don't get it!" he exclaimed. "It's like none of the others can see what Anansi's up to! They all think he's the best thing that's ever happened. Why can't they see the truth? It's just so obvious!"

"Whaaaat?" squawked Betsy quietly.

"Of course, it's obvious!" exclaimed Jack, looking over to Lily.

"I'm with Betsy," said Lily. "After all, you don't know for *sure* that he's a troll spy. Why don't you just try being friends with him? Then you could ask him what's going on."

Jack snorted loudly. "What, *friends*? With Anansi? He's a spy. I saw him talking to that troll in the woods, *remember*?"

"If he *really* was a troll," said Lily, "or working *with* the trolls, don't you think he'd have done something by now?"

"**Whaaat...**" agreed Betsy, nodding her head.

"So, you're both on his side now too! Is that it?"

"Don't be silly!" replied Lily. "It's just, well, I've spent a long time not having many friends myself." She looked a bit sad. "Apart from you, I don't really have any *normal* friends, so I feel a little sorry for this boy—all on his own, miles away from home…"

"He. Is. A. Troll. Spy!" stated Jack.

"And that's all there is to it."

"You're going to start running out of memories if you keep buying spells, Jack!" said Lily sadly. "Why not quit while you're ahead?"

"But I'm not ahead, am I?" said Jack. "So I would like to buy another spell please, if you'd be so kind."

Lily rolled her eyes. "I suppose you could try a magic mirror. I've got one that reveals the true nature of whoever looks into it."

"Perfect!" Jack grinned. "I'll take it!"

Jack was flying a kite with his mom and dad up on the big hill outside Tale Town. His parents were arm in arm and smiling. Jack looked up at them and felt a warm glow inside. A strong gust of wind suddenly swept down, snapping the string and carrying the kite far out to sea. Jack felt a pang of sadness, then his dad smiled and took an old handkerchief out of his pocket. He bound it to some twigs and reattached it to the broken string. Moments later, the makeshift kite was dancing in the sky once more.

For a moment, the memory lingered in Jack's mind, then it vanished as though it had never been there.

Jack cackled to himself as he waited for Red, Anansi, and the others to walk past. The cackle had caught him by surprise. Now that he'd heard himself doing so, he felt uncomfortable. It was a bit like a normal laugh, but with all the fun and enjoyment sucked out of it. It wasn't a nice sound.

Betsy looked at Jack for a long time. She didn't say anything, but somehow Jack could tell that she wasn't happy.

"What?" he asked, but Betsy just bent down to peck at the floor angrily.

After a short wait, Jack saw his friends walking toward him. Lily had wrapped the mirror up so he didn't acciden- tally reveal anyone else's true nature to them. Just as Anansi was getting close, Jack pulled out the mirror…but he was holding it the wrong way.

Staring back at Jack from the mirror's glassy surface was a boy with red hair. At first glance the boy looked just like him. Then, as Jack looked closer, he noticed a cold, hard glint in the boy's tired eyes. The boy stared back at Jack with such sad loneliness that Jack gasped. Was that really him?

"Jack!" Anansi's voice rang out. "What are you doing?"

As Jack spun around, the mirror slipped from his fingers and fell to the floor, shattering into tiny pieces.

"Are you all right?" asked Anansi, rushing over to help.

Jack shooed him away and tried to pick

up some pieces, desperate to see if they would still work, but all the jagged shards reflected now was a normal scene.

"Jack!" Anansi said quietly, bending down to look Jack in the eye. "I don't know what you're up to, but I *do* know a magic mirror when I see one."

Jack's eyes widened as Anansi continued, "Whatever it is that you *think* you know, I'd just forget about it if I were you."

Jack jumped up angrily. "You might have *them* fooled!" he snarled, nodding at Red and the others. "But not me!"

Then he turned and ran off, with Betsy flapping after him.

9

The Spell Thief

$\mathcal{J}$ ack sat on his bed and sulked. Usually
Betsy would curl up at his feet, but
today she seemed to be in a bad mood
and had gone off somewhere. He looked
around his bedroom. So much of it seemed
strange to him. Propped up in the corner
was a tattered old kite that looked like
it had been made out of a handkerchief
and some twigs. There were lots of other
things that he couldn't remember having

seen before too: a hand-carved wooden boat, a collection of dried leaves. Where had all this junk come from?

Jack stormed out, throwing the old kite in the trash as he went. He didn't know where Betsy was, and he didn't care. All he was thinking about was getting another spell from Lily, something that would *actually* work this time…

The last of the whirlpool faded away in a froth of bubbles, leaving Jack floating in Lily's underwater cavern.

"Hey, Jack!" beamed Lily, doing a somersault as she swam over toward him. "It's lovely to see you again so soon! Where's Betsy?"

"Not sure," replied Jack.

"So, how did the mirror work?"

"Not so great, really. I dropped it."

"Well, I did try to warn you. Most sea witch spells are unpredictable," Lily replied. "Anyway, I've been thinking—"

"Me too!" interrupted Jack.

"What a coincidence!" exclaimed Lily, clapping her hands. "*That's* why I like you, Jack. We are *so* on the same wavelength!"

"Don't most people think?" asked Jack, looking confused.

"Not like we do!" Lily said with a grin.

"Shall we see if we've been thinking the same thing?"

"OK!" said Jack, smiling a little. Lily always seemed to cheer him up. "After a count of three, let's both say our thoughts. One, two, *three*…"

They spoke at the same time—but they said very different things.

Lily said, "I want to give you a spell, for free! A spell that would mean you and Betsy could come and explore the ocean with me! I could show you all my favorite places. It'll be *loads* of fun!"

But Jack said, "Do you have a spell that would turn Anansi into a troll? I know it's kind of cheating, but once Red and the others see him like that, then they'll *have* to believe me!"

There was silence.

"Oh. Right. I see. That again…" said Lily in a flat, cold voice.

"I'd love to come exploring with you…another time? You know?" said Jack. "It's just I'm kind of busy with the whole Anansi thing."

Lily sighed. "He's not a troll spy, Jack. He's a boy, an ordinary boy, just like *you*!"

"He can talk to spiders!" said Jack.

"Well, you know, ordinary for around here!" snapped Lily. "Look at me, for goodness sake!" She swished her tail through the water. "Either way, the answer is no. There *are* spells that can change people into anything you want," Lily said, pointing at a shelf of bloodred jars. "But they're nasty ones—really nasty—and I bet it would all go wrong anyway!"

"Yeah, but—"

"But *nothing*!" shouted Lily. It was the first time Jack had seen her angry. Her eyes flashed a bright green, and her hair swirled around her like fire. "I thought that you had come here to see *me*, but all you care about is being mean to that boy. I'm not even sure I want to be friends with you anymore!"

A long, uncomfortable silence stretched out between them.

"I think you should go," said Lily. "Good-bye, Jack." She swam angrily past him and out of the cave.

The whirlpool started swirling, ready to drag Jack back up toward the surface.

As Jack floated past the row of red jars that Lily had pointed at, his arm shot out and grabbed one. He knew that what he was doing was bad. Really, *really* bad. But he just couldn't help himself. Before he could change his mind, he was pulled into the center of the swirling whirlpool and dragged toward the surface.

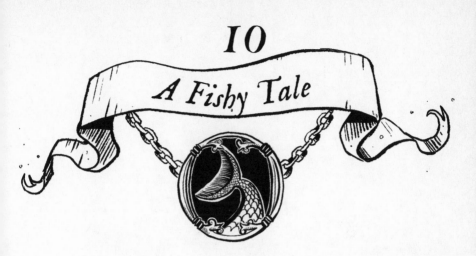

IO

A Fishy Tale

*O*nce Jack was back in town, he found a quiet alleyway and carefully opened the jar to see what was inside. There was a slight hiss, and the air was filled with the stink of burning hair. Jack peered in to see a mysterious dusty substance swirling around within the jar. Just looking at it made Jack's stomach feel funny.

He also realized he had no idea how

the spell worked and there was no way
that he could ask Lily now.

He was still peering into the jar when
a shrill voice shrieked, "What have you
got in that jar, you ghastly creature?"

Jack spun around, hastily slamming the
lid shut. "Nothing!" he gasped as a
wicked stepmother stalked toward him
like a two-legged grasshopper in a dress.

"Nothing, eh?" sneered the wicked

stepmother unpleasantly. "What sort of nothing does a grubby little thing like you need to keep hidden then?"

"A *private* sort of nothing," replied Jack, more bravely than he felt.

"Oh-ho! A private sort of…" Then the wicked stepmother stopped. Her paper-thin nostrils quivered as she tried to pluck a scent out of the air. "I can smell magic! *Strong* magic!"

Jack started to feel even more nervous.

"Now correct me if I'm wrong, *dearie*…" The stepmother's voice suddenly turned soft, as if she had been gargling with honey and golden syrup. "But might that be a sea witch's spell?"

"Maaaybe?" replied Jack, feeling out of his depth.

"A spell of changing? Hmm, yes?"

"Perhaps…"

"Such a wonderful spell!" exclaimed the stepmother wistfully. "I remember turning my third ex-husband's new wife into a cake using that spell! Of course, it didn't last very long, just a couple of hours—just long enough for her family to get hungry!"

Jack shuddered.

"All I had to do was think of a cake. So simple, not like the complicated spells you get nowadays!"

"What? You just thought of a cake, and she turned into one?" asked Jack.

"No, you simpleminded peasant!" hissed the stepmother. "I had to cover her in the dust first!" Her voice changed again. "Now, if you'd be so kind as to hand over that jar…" She approached Jack slowly, her sharp fingernails clawing toward him as she reached for the spell.

"Come on, *dearie*…" cooed the stepmother. "Hand it over…"

Jack backed away from her, shaking his head.

"*Now!*" shrieked the stepmother.

Jack didn't have time to think. He scooped his hand into the jar and flung a handful of dust at the stepmother's head. He tried to think of something to turn her into, but his mind had gone blank. Then, out of the corner of his mind popped a thought. It was a very silly thought, and he hadn't even *really* meant to think it, but now he had...

Mushroom.

WHUMPH!

There was a flash of black light accompanied by the nostril-burning smell of rotten eggs and mustard powder. When the thick, oily smoke had cleared, Jack was met with a very strange sight.

The wicked stepmother was still standing there, but now she had a mushroom for a head.

"Whaaaat?!?" yelled Jack.

The stepmother raised her hands to where her face should be. She obviously didn't like what her hands discovered. Her whole body quivered in shock, and then she leaped into the air and tried to run off, but kept tripping over. After all, mushrooms don't have any eyes.

———◆———

Ten minutes later, Jack was sneaking along silently behind Anansi and Red, who were on their own. All he needed to do was wait until Red wasn't watching, sprinkle Anansi with the dust, and think "troll." It was going to be easy!

It wasn't long before Jack saw his chance. Red and Anansi were coming up to the old wooden footbridge that crossed over the River Tale. It was so narrow that only one person could cross at a time, and Red had gone first. Jack sneaked up behind Anansi, silently opening the jar. "Troll…troll…troll," he repeated in his head. He dipped his hand into the jar and took a deep breath. "Here goes…"

Suddenly the water below the bridge erupted into a furious explosion of spray. Lily's head and shoulders appeared, her face set into a cold, hard expression.

"*Jack!*" she shouted, her voice thick with anger.

Jack's hand jerked out and threw the dust high into the air, well over Anansi's head, to settle in a cloud all over Red.

"Lily?" Jack yelped. Then, with a horrible sinking feeling, he realized what he'd done.

WHUMPH!

There was silence as everyone peered at the cloud of thick, ugly smoke where Red had been standing.

As the smoke cleared, everyone looked on in shock. Flapping around on the bridge was Red. But she *looked* just like Lily, including her long, curling fish tail.

"What's happened?" shrieked Red, in Lily's

voice. "I can't feel my legs!" She looked down at her tail and said nothing for a moment. Then she screamed—very loudly, and for an awfully long time.

"How could you steal from me, Jack?" shouted the real Lily. "I thought we were friends?"

"We *were*... I mean, we *are*!" cried Jack. "It's just..."

"And what about me?" demanded Red. "I'm half-fish! It's just too weird!" She glanced over at Lily in the river and added, "No offense."

"None taken."

"I-I-I'm sorry!" stammered Jack. "I didn't mean—"

"Oh, just be quiet, Jack!" shouted Red and Lily at the same time.

A terrible feeling of shame

burned up within Jack. Tears streamed from his eyes, and he ran away as fast as he could.

He'd made a mess of everything and upset *all* his friends. Now there was no way that he'd be able to stop whatever it was that Anansi was planning with the trolls. Jack ran blindly on. He didn't care where he was going, as long as it was somewhere else.

II

A New Friend

*T*he air smelled damp and felt cold. Above Jack's head, bare branches intertwined like bony fingers and a miserable-looking group of toads croaked an unhappy chorus. It was the most miserable song you could imagine.

Jack was in Despair.

Despair was a strange place. You couldn't set out to find Despair—it found you. Jack had been there only once before, when his dad had first gone away to mine the Moonstone. Jack frowned. For some reason he couldn't remember *any* happy memories about his dad…and that made him feel even worse.

Everything had gone wrong. All his friends were mad at him, even Betsy. He'd ruined things with Lily, and because of him, Red was going to be a mermaid for…well, he didn't even know for how long!

The sound of a branch snapping got his attention. *What was that?* He listened carefully. There were more branches snapping and a quiet sobbing. *Someone was coming!*

Jack moved silently toward the bushes

to hide. He peered through the yellowed leaves and had to stop himself from gasping out loud when he saw Anansi approaching—with the troll!

Anansi sat down heavily on a tree stump and started to cry more loudly.

The troll sighed a deep, heavy sigh and laid a weighty arm on Anansi's shoulders.

"It'll be all right, Anansi…" said the troll. "You'll see."

"Will it though, Uncle Rufaro?" replied Anansi. "Dad said it would be *all right* when he sent me here. He said that if I could get you the Moonstone potion it would fix everything. But you're still cursed to look like a troll, which means Mom will be too!"

"I know," said the troll. "But we've got to keep hoping, haven't we?"

"But what if we can't find out who cast the spell?" exclaimed Anansi. "If we can't, then you'll have to spend the rest of your lives looking like trolls. You'll always be on the run, always hiding away." Anansi sniffed.

"Shhh," comforted the troll. "Look, I know the potion didn't work. Believe me, I'm just as upset as you—but as soon as we find out who cursed us, we'll be able to fix it. It's just going to take a little more time than we thought."

"And until then, you, Mom, Nana, and Grandpa are all going to look like trolls?"

"I'm afraid so. But at least they're all together back home. It's just me who has to hide away in these creepy woods with only a few crazy imps for company!"

"Hey!" exclaimed an angry voice as an imp glared out through a bush at them. "Imps have feelings too!"

"Yes, of course…sorry!" said Rufaro.

A queasy feeling rushed through Jack as he began to realize that he might have gotten things a *teeny* bit wrong.

"I'm sorry," sniffed Anansi. "I can normally deal with things better than this."

"There's nothing wrong with feeling sad, Anansi," said his uncle. "But don't worry. I'll get your mom back to normal as soon as possible—and me and the rest of the family too!"

The queasy feeling inside Jack turned into a rush of sickness. There was something he needed to say. He scrambled awkwardly out of the bushes.

"You!" gasped Anansi. "What are you doing here?"

"I…er…well…"

"*What?*" shouted Anansi. "Do you want to make me even more unhappy?"

"No!" protested Jack. "It's not like that!"

Anansi stared at him coldly and said nothing.

Jack took a deep breath. He'd done some difficult and dangerous things in his time (it's not everyone that has the courage to sneak into a giant's castle while it's singing creepy songs about smelling your blood), but this—*this*—was the hardest thing he'd ever had to do.

Jack let out his breath slowly and said, "I'm sorry, Anansi."

There was silence. Anansi looked surprised. He opened his mouth to speak and then closed it again. Jack found that now that he'd started, the words came out a lot easier. "I'm sorry I thought you were a troll spy. I was wrong. And I'm sorry I was so mean to you. I know it doesn't make it any better, but I really *did* think you were a spy. I'll understand if you hate me and never want to see me again, but I just wanted you to know. OK?"

The silence carried on. Anansi looked at Jack. Eventually he spoke. "Jack. I *am* a troll spy."

"Whaaaaat!?!" Jack gasped.

"I'm just joking!" Anansi said, then he and his uncle burst out laughing. "Sorry, I just couldn't help myself!"

"That was *mean*, Anansi!" said Rufaro. "But very funny."

A smile pulled at the corner of Jack's mouth, dragging it upward until he couldn't resist it any longer and joined in.

As they carried on laughing, nobody noticed the spindly branches above their heads disappearing. The toads all hopped off somewhere else as shoots of grass sprang up through the muddy ground. Brightly colored flowers dotted the clearing as leaves sprouted on the bushes and trees.

"I should say sorry too," said Anansi. "I knew you'd seen me talking with the imp, but I lied about it. I just didn't want anyone to know what had happened to Mom and my uncle." Anansi nodded at the troll next to him. "You know, people get all *Argghh, it's a troll!* But now that you know…Jack, meet Rufaro. Rufaro, meet Jack."

Rufaro held out one huge hand, and Jack tentatively shook it.

"Please excuse my appearance…" said Rufaro, indicating his ill-fitting troll clothes. "I'm a bit behind on my laundry."

"And his bathing!" whispered Anansi.

"I heard that!" muttered Rufaro.

"So what happened?" asked Jack. "With the, you know, troll thing?"

Rufaro sighed. "My whole family has been cursed. It was nearly a year ago now. There was a huge storm. I was running for shelter when a bolt of lightning shot down and struck me. When I woke up, I was like this."

"And you don't know who did it or why?"

"No." Rufaro shook his head, "But I

will find out, Jack. Believe me, I will. And when I do, I'll find a way to fix this."

"Let me know if you need any help," said Jack, looking at Anansi. "It's the least I could do."

Rufaro slapped Jack on the back, making his teeth rattle. "You're a good lad, Jack! I never believed all those terrible things that Anansi said about you!"

Anansi smiled awkwardly at Jack. "That was, er...*before*, wasn't it? So, does this make us friends then?"

"I'd like that," said Jack. "I'd like that a lot."

Jack and Anansi walked back toward Tale Town together. Rufaro wasn't coming with them. Mainly because he still looked (and smelled) like a troll.

"Hey, Anansi," Jack said, feeling rather sheepish. "Is Red still, *you know*, half-fish?"

Anansi shook his head. "The spell didn't last very long, although I'm not sure Red would see it that way."

Jack squirmed uncomfortably. He imagined how angry Red was going to be with him. Still, at least she was back to normal now. That just left one problem to fix. "Anansi, do you want to come to the beach with me?" asked Jack.

"Sure," replied Anansi. "As long as it doesn't involve magic. Or trolls!"

Jack grinned. "No trolls, but maybe a *bit* of magic. Come on, I'll show you!"

12

Happily Ever After?

I don't understand!" exclaimed Jack, as he looked all over the beach for a swan-shaped stone. "I can normally find one easily."

"I guess Lily was, um, a bit *annoyed* with you?" said Anansi carefully.

"That's why it's so important I see her!" insisted Jack. He carried on searching for a while, but it was hopeless.

Jack waded out purposefully into the sea.

"What are you doing?" called Anansi from the shore.

"Lily!" Jack yelled. "Lily!" He waded farther out. The waves beat him back, but each time he was knocked off his feet he scrambled up again.

"Lily!" he shouted again. "If you can hear me, *please* come up. There's something I have to say to you!"

There was no response.

"I'm sorry, all right?" shouted Jack. "I was an idiot. And…and a bad friend. I've brought someone to meet you. I think you'll be surprised when you see who it is."

"Well?" said Lily's voice from directly behind him.

Jack spun around, lost his footing, and splashed into the sea.

"I see you're about as graceful on land as you are in the water," said Lily.

"Look, I'm sorry," replied Jack. "I've been an idiot, and I can see that now."

"You *stole* from me, Jack."

"I know," said Jack. "I don't have an excuse for anything that I did. It was all really bad. But I've made up with Anansi now, and I really hope that we can be friends again too."

"*You're* friends with *Anansi*?" spluttered Lily.

Jack nodded toward the other boy standing out on the beach. Anansi waved.

"Well," said Lily, "I didn't see *that* coming!"

"And I want to give you something," said Jack. "Another happy memory."

"That won't pay for the spell you stole, Jack," replied Lily.

"I know," said Jack. "I'll find a way to make that up to you, I promise. But, *please*, let me just give you this memory. It's my happiest in a long time."

Lily rolled her eyes. "Go on then," she said.

Jack concentrated. He thought back to the first time he'd met Lily. How funny she was and how much she'd made him laugh. He couldn't even get halfway through the memory before Lily grabbed him in a huge, very wet hug.

"Oh, Jack!" she said happily. "That is *literally* the nicest thing that anyone has

done for me in the last three minutes! But I won't keep that one. In fact, I wasn't going to keep any of the others either. I know how much you miss your dad. I couldn't take those memories from you."

Jack felt the strangest sensation, as though someone was shuffling a deck of cards inside his brain. "Whoa!" he exclaimed as everything settled down again inside his head.

"Now," said Lily with a grin, "how about I take you and Anansi on a tour of the ocean?"

Jack looked over at Anansi. "What do you think?" he asked.

"Let me see…" replied Anansi. "How about…*yes!*"

———————◆———————

Red was snoozing against the Story Tree while Rapunzel and the twins lounged nearby. Betsy flapped and lightly pecked at Red's feet.

"Whaaat?!" exclaimed Red in surprise. **"Whaʌaat?!"** screeched Betsy.

"Uh, no, sorry, Bets, I don't know

where he is," replied Red. "And to be honest, I don't really care!"

"**Whaaat...**" squawked Betsy.

"I know it's not *your* fault," said Red, stroking the hen. "But I *am* really mad at Jack right now."

She lay back against the tree while the twins argued about which was the better color—blue or green. She was just starting to get over the horror of having spent the whole afternoon in a fishpond when Rapunzel asked quietly, "So, what was it like being a mermaid?"

Red opened her eyes. "I told you," she growled. "I *don't* want to talk about it."

"I know!" said Rapunzel. "But, I mean, it must have been—"

"I said I *do not* want to talk about it!"

Rapunzel had just opened her mouth to speak again when Hansel and Gretel interrupted her. "Look! Here comes Anansi—"

"—and Jack!"

Red and Rapunzel spun around.

Walking along the pathway, soaking wet and chattering away like they'd known each other for years, were Anansi and Jack.

"What about that cave where every-thing glowed in the dark?" exclaimed Anansi.

"And who'd have thought an octopus would know so many great jokes?" added Jack.

"I'm sorry?" said Red, shaking her head. "Last time I checked you two were bitter enemies and now, well, now *this*." She pointed at the two of them.

"**Whaaaat?**" added Betsy.

Jack sighed. "Do you want the long version or the short one?"

The twins, Red, and Rapunzel looked at each other.

"Let's go for short," said Rapunzel.

"OK," replied Jack. "Well, it goes a little like this: I was an idiot. I let you all

down, and I owe you"—
he looked at Red—"a
huge apology."

Red glared at Jack.

Anansi stepped in.
"Honestly, Red, if I have to
hear Jack apologize to another
person today, I think I'll have to
eat my own ears! You wouldn't want me
to eat my own ears, would you?"

A hint of a smile curled around Red's
mouth.

"You'd have to help me," continued
Anansi. "There's no way I could eat
them while they're still attached to my
head, and they seem to be pretty well
stuck on." He tugged at his ears.

Red smiled, even though she was still trying to feel angry.

"OK," said Anansi, "if that's how it's got to be. Red, if you grab this one and Rapunzel takes the other it shouldn't take us too long. So, on a count of three, you pull, OK? One, two…"

"All right!" exclaimed Red. "You can keep your stupid ears, Anansi. We'll find you something else to eat if you're *that* hungry!"

"So, are we OK?" asked Jack.

"As long as you're going to stop acting like an idiot, then *yes*, we're OK," replied Red.

"Great!" said Rapunzel. "But there's just one thing I'm still curious about…"

Everyone turned to look at her.

"I'd *still* like to know how it feels to be a mermaid!"

Red's eyes narrowed when Betsy suddenly squawked, **"WHAAAAAT!?!"** and pointed a wing upward. Growing delicately out of the Story Tree was a shining silver stem. It curled around in the afternoon sunlight, and a small golden leaf appeared at the end of it.

"It looks like your adventure's made it on to the Story Tree!" exclaimed Red excitedly. "You'll always be a part of Tale Town now, Anansi."

"Well, hopefully that's just the beginning!" he replied, smiling.

13

A Homecoming

*T*ime passed quickly, and before long, Anansi's vacation was over and it was time for him to return home. Once again, they all went up to Lookout Point to watch the boat sail in, but this time there was no racing and no excitement.

"Maybe we could come and visit you?" said Jack sadly, even though they all knew there was no way that they'd be allowed to go to Far Far Away on their own.

"Or maybe you could have another—"

"—vacation here?" added Hansel and Gretel.

Eventually Red said, "I think I can see the ship."

Everyone peered out to sea. Jack watched as it crept closer and closer. Then he gasped. He scooped up Betsy and sprinted down the path toward the dock.

"What's going on?" called Rapunzel.

"I'm not sure," shouted Jack. "But I *think* I saw my dad on deck!"

———•◆•———

By the time Jack and the others arrived at the dock, the ship was starting to unload. Jack watched as a stream of travelers poured off the boat, carrying luggage and talking of the exciting times they'd had. The stream of people became a trickle, and then, eventually, there was no one left.

"Maybe it was just someone who looked like your dad?" said Anansi.

"Maybe," said Jack quietly. "But I could have *sworn* it was him."

"I'm sorry, Jack." Red placed a hand on her friend's shoulder. "Shall we help Anansi get his things?"

As they turned to leave, a grating creak rang out. A huge door was opening on the boat. A ramp slid out until it rested on the docks, then a team of people started to unload some heavy-looking machinery.

Jack blinked in surprise. There, right in front of him, helping another man heave a huge drill down onto the dockside was his father.

"Dad!" he yelled as loud as he could, sprinting forward. "*Dad!*"

"*Dad!*" shouted Anansi at the same time.

Jack and Anansi shot a look over at each other and stopped dead in their tracks.

"We…we…*have the same dad*?" gasped Jack.

Anansi burst out laughing. "No!" he said when he could finally speak again. "My dad is the *other* man!"

"Ah! Yeah. Of course," replied Jack. "I knew that all along! But what's he doing here? What are they both doing here?"

"What? You're not happy to see me?" called out Jack's father as he walked over, a big grin spread across his face.

"Of course I am!" said Jack. "It's just…I don't understand?"

"Let me tell you a story," replied his dad, smiling.

"What...now?"

"Once upon a time..." began Jack's father. "Well, about three months ago, one of the Fairy Tale Kingdom's more accident-prone princes was heading out on a quest, when he fell down a deep crack in the ground. As he explored farther it led on to a huge underground chamber... lined entirely with Moonstone!"

Everybody gasped. Jack's father smiled broadly. "Nobody could tell how much Moonstone was hidden in there, so a mining team was sent home to find out. And that's where Abioye and I come into it." He nodded at Anansi's father.

"You and Anansi's dad know each

other?" asked Jack, his mouth hanging open.

"We've been friends for years!" replied Jack's dad, clapping Abioye on the shoulder.

"Not at first though!" added Abioye. "There were a few, um, *misunderstandings* when we first met."

"All water under a troll's bridge now!" said Jack's dad. "I hope you've made Anansi feel at home, Jack?"

"Um…" said Jack.

"There's nowhere else I'd rather be," said Anansi quickly.

"Well, that's good!" said Abioye. "Because we're going to be living here as long as there's Moonstone to mine."

"Really?" exclaimed Anansi.

"Really," said his father.

"And what about Mom?" said Anansi. "Is she…"

"She'll be coming too," said Abioye. "But there are a few things I need to sort out first, OK?"

Anansi nodded.

"Anyway, we've been at sea for nearly three months!" said Jack's dad. "I'd like something to eat that isn't dried, smoked, or salted. Who wants to go to Greentop's? My treat!"

Jack smiled as everyone chattered excitedly. His dad was here—to stay! Anansi was moving to Tale Town. The world seemed perfect.

Who knew what adventures lay ahead?

Jack

Strengths: Running (especially running away from giants that want to grind his bones into flour).

Weaknesses: Pride and just a teeny, tiny touch of jealousy.

Likes: His pet hen, Betsy; golden eggs; playing with his friends; and having fun.

Dislikes: Being told what to do and calling his teacher "Mom" accidentally.

Lily

Strengths: Breathing underwater (a pretty vital skill if you happen to live in the ocean).

Weaknesses: Riding a bike-not that there are bikes underwater anyway.

Likes: Everything! Lily is the most positive sea witch you will ever meet!

Dislikes: Having to be mean to people since she's meant to be a sea witch.

Betsy

Strengths: Talking (it's unbelievably rare for a hen to be able to talk, so you'd better be impressed).

Weaknesses: Saying any word other than "What!"

Likes: Jack, pecking at the ground, eating grain, dining out, and long walks on the beach.

Dislikes: The color purple and foxes. Especially foxes!

Anansi

Strengths: Speaking with spiders, climbing up spiderwebs, finding spiders—just anything to do with spiders.

Weaknesses: Sometimes Anansi has to fib to protect his family's secret.

Likes: Spiders (naturally!), telling incredible stories. and playing tricks on people.

Dislikes: Really clean houses where all the cobwebs have been dusted away.

The adventure continues in

TOM PERCIVAL

Little
Legends

·THE· GREAT TROLL RESCUE

I
A Storm Brewing

*R*ed, Anansi, Rapunzel, Jack, and his magical talking hen, Betsy, were sitting beneath the leafy branches of the Story Tree in the middle of Tale Town.

The afternoon sun beat down on them, and the air was thick and heavy. Out to sea, storm clouds were gathering. The nice weather wouldn't last for long.

"What do you think Hansel and Gretel are up to?" asked Red.

"They said they were going camping with their dad," said Rapunzel.

"Whaaaat?" squawked Betsy, rolling her eyes. Although she was a talking hen, Betsy could only say the word **"What"** —but somehow her friends always knew what she meant.

Jack frowned. "It is *weird*, isn't it?" he said. "They go off on these trips to the woods with their dad, and then we don't see them for weeks! But I saw their dad in town just this morning with *another* new wife—and she's even worse than the last one. He was buying her a diamond-covered toilet-paper holder and looked *really* miserable."

They fell silent. Life in Tale Town was always *slightly* unusual, but what else

would you expect
in a place where
stories   literally
grew on trees?

The Story Tree
was the reason that
Tale Town got its
name. On its branches
grew every story that had ever been told
near it. To "read" the stories, all you
had to do was run your finger along any
branch or leaf and the tale would spring
to life in your head. All the children had
at least one or two stories growing on the
Story Tree—even Anansi, who hadn't
been living there very long.

"So, Anansi, how's your uncle Rufaro
doing?" asked Rapunzel. "Any news?"

"Well, he still looks like a troll," replied Anansi. "So he's still living in that stinking cave in the woods, away from all his friends and family, surviving on scraps of food and water from that smelly pond."

"Hmm," replied Rapunzel. "So not that great, then?"

"Not really," said Anansi with a sigh.

It had been well over a year since almost all of Anansi's family had been cursed to look, sound, and smell like trolls. Only Anansi and his father still looked human. Nobody knew how it had happened or why. More worrisome, nobody had the slightest clue how to turn them back. *Even* more worrisome, the people of Tale Town and the trolls had been at war for as long as anyone could remember. Without a cure, his family would never be able to come home.

"And what about your mom?" asked Jack. "Is she still on her way here?"

Anansi brightened. "Yeah, she should arrive any day now! Dad got her a ticket on a boat from Far Far Away." He paused. "Well, I say a 'ticket'… Let's just say she's on a boat."

"Don't worry, Anansi," said Red, patting him on the arm. "I just know that Rufaro will be able to find a cure."

"I guess so," replied Anansi, but he didn't sound hopeful.

A large raindrop landed with a puff

of dust on the dry ground, and Jack glanced up.

"Looks like it's about to—"

He was interrupted by a crash of thunder as huge, fat raindrops fell all around them. Everybody sprang to their feet and ran for cover.

———◆◆———

The captain had already given the order to abandon ship. The boat had been thrown on to a series of jagged rocks a mile or so from Tale Town and was filling with water. As the last of the lifeboats were lowered, a deep voice boomed from a huge box in storage.

"Hello? Is there anybody there? I don't want to alarm you, but my feet are getting wet, and I just wondered if everything was OK? The boat's not sinking, is it?"

There was no response. By now water was halfway up the side of the crate that was printed with the words:

TAKE CARE.
ENCHANTED
SPINNING WHEELS –
MAY CAUSE DROWSINESS

"*Yiiikes!*" squealed the voice as the water rose higher.

It was hard to imagine such a deep and gravelly voice squealing, but *somehow* it managed it.

"I'm going to come out now," the voice continued. "But just to warn you...I look a *teeny* bit like a troll. But I'm not *really* a troll! So, no spears or swords, OK? Agreed?"

Again there was no answer.

The voice in the box muttered, "Here we go then," and with a crash the crate exploded outward, revealing a very large, very trolly-looking *troll*.

The troll glanced around and realized that the ship definitely *was* sinking. It searched through its pockets until it found what it was looking for—a bright-yellow bottle—then it scrambled up the steps toward the deck and leaped up the mast, climbing as fast as it could until it reached the crow's nest. Shutting its eyes in concentration, the troll whispered a spell into the yellow bottle, then sealed it with a cork and flung it far out into the towering waves.

Seconds later, the troll fell into the churning water, leaving a splash of white spray that was immediately swallowed up in the darkness of the storm.

2
Message in a Bottle

*T*he next day, all anyone could talk about was the shipwreck. Red, Jack, Rapunzel, Anansi, and Betsy were walking to the beach to see if anything exciting had washed up.

Red shuddered. "I'm glad everyone made it back to shore," she said. "It must have been terrifying!"

"I know!" exclaimed Rapunzel, stroking her incredibly long braids. "Imagine having to wash all that saltwater out of your hair!"

"That's not *exactly* what I meant," began Red, but before she had a chance to finish, Old Bert wheeled his cart around the corner. Red groaned. She didn't like seafood at the best of times, and Old Bert's seafood snack cart smelled *very* fishy.

"Mornin', small fry!" Old Bert said

with a toothy grin. "Which of me salty snacks will you be 'avin' today?"

Red looked around and realized her friends had vanished as quickly as Old Bert had appeared. She could see Jack's feet poking out from underneath a bush, while Betsy was pretending to be the figurehead on a boat.

"The thing is," replied Red, "I've only just had breakfast, so I'm, er, kind of full."

Old Bert chuckled. "Always room for a pot of me finest squid rings!" he said, pulling out a grubby jar.

"*Ewwww!*" exclaimed Red. "I mean, erm, I don't have enough money."

Bert's eyes narrowed. "Well, I do 'ave some old fish tails going cheap—not even rotten yet. How many d'yer want?"

"Yes, *but*, I'm allergic to fish tails!"

"*Really?*" asked Bert, his needle-sharp eyes boring into her. "Just last week I sold you eight of 'em!"

"I know!" continued Red, shivering at the memory. "I think that was what did it."

A cunning smile stretched across Bert's face. "As it happens I'm also sellin' ice cream today," he said. "How does that grab yer?"

"Really?" asked Red, "Well, I probably *could* eat an ice cream…"

Before Red knew what had happened, all her money was gone, she was holding a wrapped ice-cream cone, and Old Bert was hobbling off whistling a tuneless sea chantey.

Red stood waiting on the path as, one by one, her friends reappeared.

"Oh, *hello*. Nice of you to join me!" she said, scowling. "I *know* you think Old Bert's always tricking me into buying some horrid seafood thing, but not today!" She waved the crumpled ice-cream cone at them triumphantly. "So *you* all missed out!"

"WHAaAT?" squawked Betsy, looking suspicious.

"Oh, come *on*, Betsy!" exclaimed Red. "Ice cream is ice cream. It'll be lovely!"

And with that she ripped off the packaging and took a huge bite.

"*GAhhhHhh!*" coughed Red. She

looked in horror at the ice cream, over to her friends, and finally at the packaging in her hand. The label was clear for everyone to see:

OLD BERT'S EEL-EYE ICE CREAM

"*Why would anyone do that?*" cried Red, throwing the ice cream in a trash can and scraping at her tongue with her fingernails.

"Red, Bert *always* tricks you into buying something, and it's *always* horrible," said Anansi. "Maybe you shouldn't be so trusting?"

Red glared at him. "If *I* hadn't trusted *you* when you first arrived in Tale Town, we wouldn't all be friends now, would we?"

Anansi looked at her. "I know," he said. "And I'm really glad you did, but—"

"Hey, look at that!" Rapunzel interrupted, pointing toward the shoreline.

Bobbing against the sand was a yellow bottle filled with a strange glowing mist. When the children got nearer, the bottle spun around until it was pointing toward them. Then it hopped up out of the sea and started rolling up the beach.

"Whoa!" said Red as the bottle came

to a stop at their feet. "It's a message in a bottle!"

"But who's it for?" wondered Jack.

They peered at the bottle and the mist inside formed into different shapes, gradually becoming clearer and clearer:

Anansi looked nervous as he bent to pick up the bottle and slowly pulled out the cork. As he did, the beach and his friends faded away. Anansi looked around in confusion. He was up in the crow's nest of a ship, late at night. Rain fell all around him, but he couldn't feel a thing. In front of him was a troll—a troll that he recognized. *It was his mother!*

Anansi tried to hug her, but his arms passed right through her.

Anansi's mother stared straight ahead and spoke quickly:

"*Anansi, my darling! The ship is sinking! I'm close to Tale Town and can see an island that I can swim to. There is a mountain on it that looks like a squirrel's nose. I'll meet you there, at the base of the mountain, where the forest ends. Come as soon as you can. I love you, Anansi. Stay safe!*"

The scene melted away, and Anansi found himself back on the beach, surrounded by his friends.

"Well?" asked Jack expectantly. "What was the message? Who was it from?"

"My mom," said Anansi. "And we need to find a boat that'll take us to Squirrel Nose Island—*right now!*"

The adventure continues! Don't miss:

About the Author

Tom Percival grew up in a remote and beautiful part of south Shropshire. It was so remote that he lived in a small trailer without electrical power or any sensible form of heating. He thinks he's probably one of the few people his age to have learned to read by the light from a gas lamp.

Having established a career as a picture book author and illustrator, *Little Legends: The Spell Thief* is Tom's first chapter book for young readers. The idea for Little Legends was developed by Tom with Made in Me, a digital studio exploring new ways for technology and storytelling to inspire the next generation.